T3-BPD-593

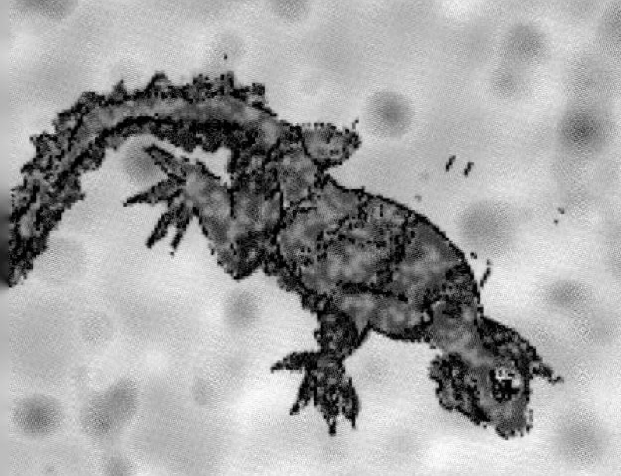

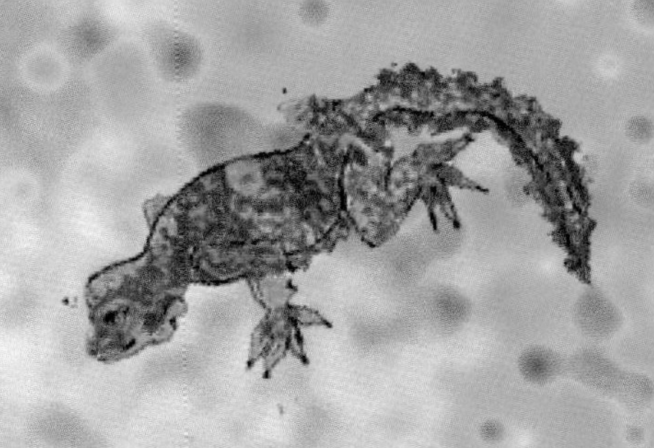

Casey's Chameleon

by Bea Alexander
Drawings by Madeleine Thomson

Book designed and painted by Bea Alexander and Jennifer Linch

Casey's Chameleon copyright © 1996 by Bea Alexander.
All rights reserved. Printed in the U.S.A.
No part of this book may be reproduced or copied in any form
without written permission from the publisher.
Bea Alexander books are published in the United States
by Kids Libris™, a division of Personal Selling Power, Inc.,
P.O. Box 5467, Fredericksburg, VA 22403, Tel. 540-752-7000.
Library of Congress Catalog Number 96-77917
ISBN # 0-939613-10-7

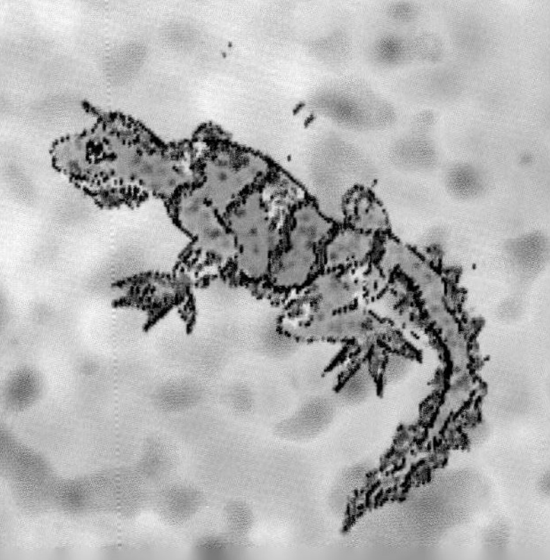

When Casey caught a chameleon that was hanging onto a dead branch, he poked some holes in the top of an old shoe box and carefully laid the chameleon and the branch in the bottom. By opening the shoe box a tiny sliver he could watch as the chameleon slowly turned its head. Casey looked at the chameleon's fat body and many colors, at its toes that were bundled together and at the long tail that curled into a big circle at the end. He watched as the eyes swiveled in different directions.

Casey had never seen anything like this chameleon before. He crept quietly into his room and placed the box at the back of his closet behind his smelliest sneakers then quickly emptied some bugs into the shoe box and closed the top again. He couldn't tell if the chameleon was going after them yet so he lay down next to the box to listen for any movement or the sound of a bug getting sucked up.

Casey lay there for about fifteen minutes but didn't hear anything. To help pass the time, he picked up a tennis ball and moved back from the closet to get in good scoring position.

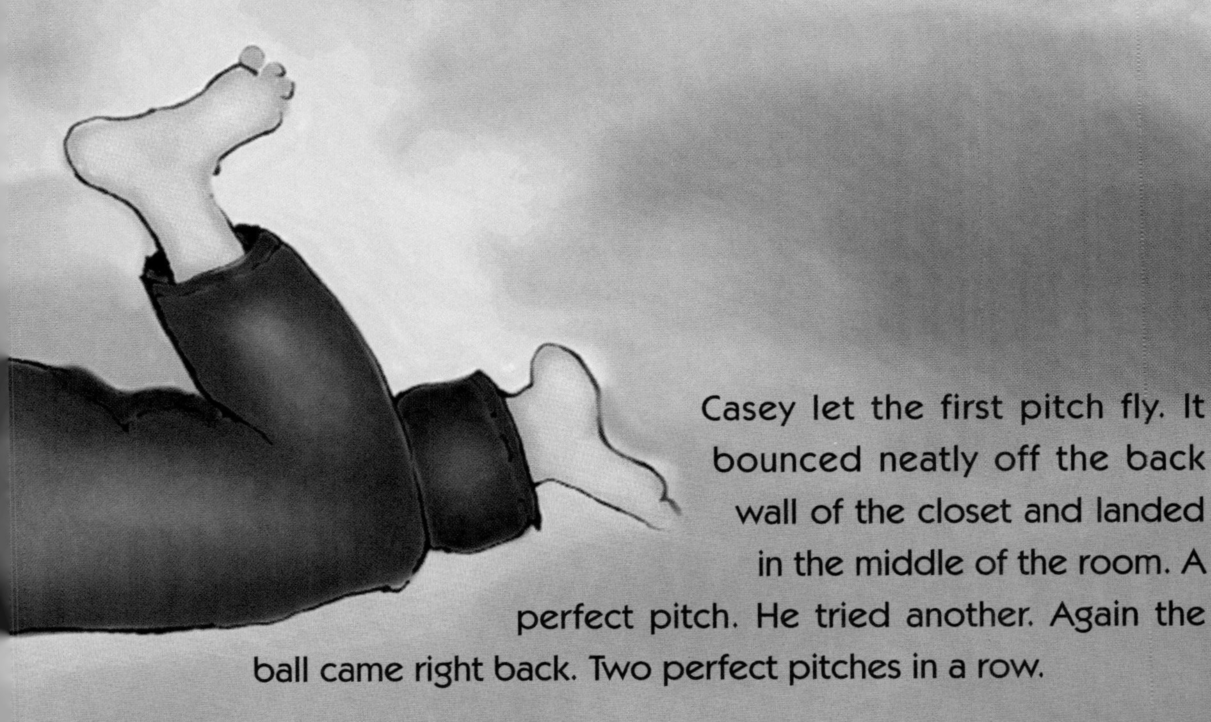

Casey let the first pitch fly. It bounced neatly off the back wall of the closet and landed in the middle of the room. A perfect pitch. He tried another. Again the ball came right back. Two perfect pitches in a row.

Casey wound up once more and aimed at the back closet wall above the shelf. This time the pitch went wild and hit the back of the closet under the shelf. It bounced off the wall before knocking off the top of the shoe box and tilting the box on its side. The ball came to a halt in one of Casey's high-top sneakers.

Just as Casey was about to check what had happened to the shoe box, his mother called for him to come right downstairs and clean up the mess he had left when he had glued his model airplane together.

By the time he got back to his room, the chameleon was out of the box and gone. Casey started a search. He looked in all his shoes, under the bed, in his bookcase, behind the dresser, in the drawers, on the window sill, behind the door and along the walls. He pulled everything out of his closet. Because he was afraid he might step on the chameleon Casey did a little dance on his toes and kept looking all around every time he moved his feet.

Next Casey looked in the hall and on the stairs, then looked in the bathroom and his parents' room.

Now Casey started to imagine what could happen to his pet. Someone could step on it. It could get smothered. It could get flushed down a toilet. It could get caught in the dishwasher. Casey looked under and behind every piece of furniture in the house. He looked all over the kitchen and in every closet. He even checked inside the refrigerator.

At dinner Casey was quiet. When his father asked about baseball practice, Casey answered something about why they didn't have stronger cages to protect the animals at the zoo. He leaned over to check under the chairs. He looked under the table, too. No chameleon.

While he was brushing his teeth, Casey checked the bathroom again. Before getting in bed he looked under the covers. His mother walked in while he was standing on a chair with a flashlight in his hand checking the back of his closet shelf. His mother told him to get right down and get in bed. Then she wanted to know why all his stuff was all over the floor and not in the closet.

He was half under the bed when his father came in to say good night. His father asked what he was doing. Casey said he had lost something. His father told him to look for it in the morning.

That night Casey dreamt about chameleons as big as dinosaurs. They tromped over an entire city stepping on baseball bats and gloves and houses. They rested on rooftops and then they all shrank to the size of small toads and people stepped on their toes. Casey woke up in a sweat. He felt for his flashlight and checked the walls all around his room.

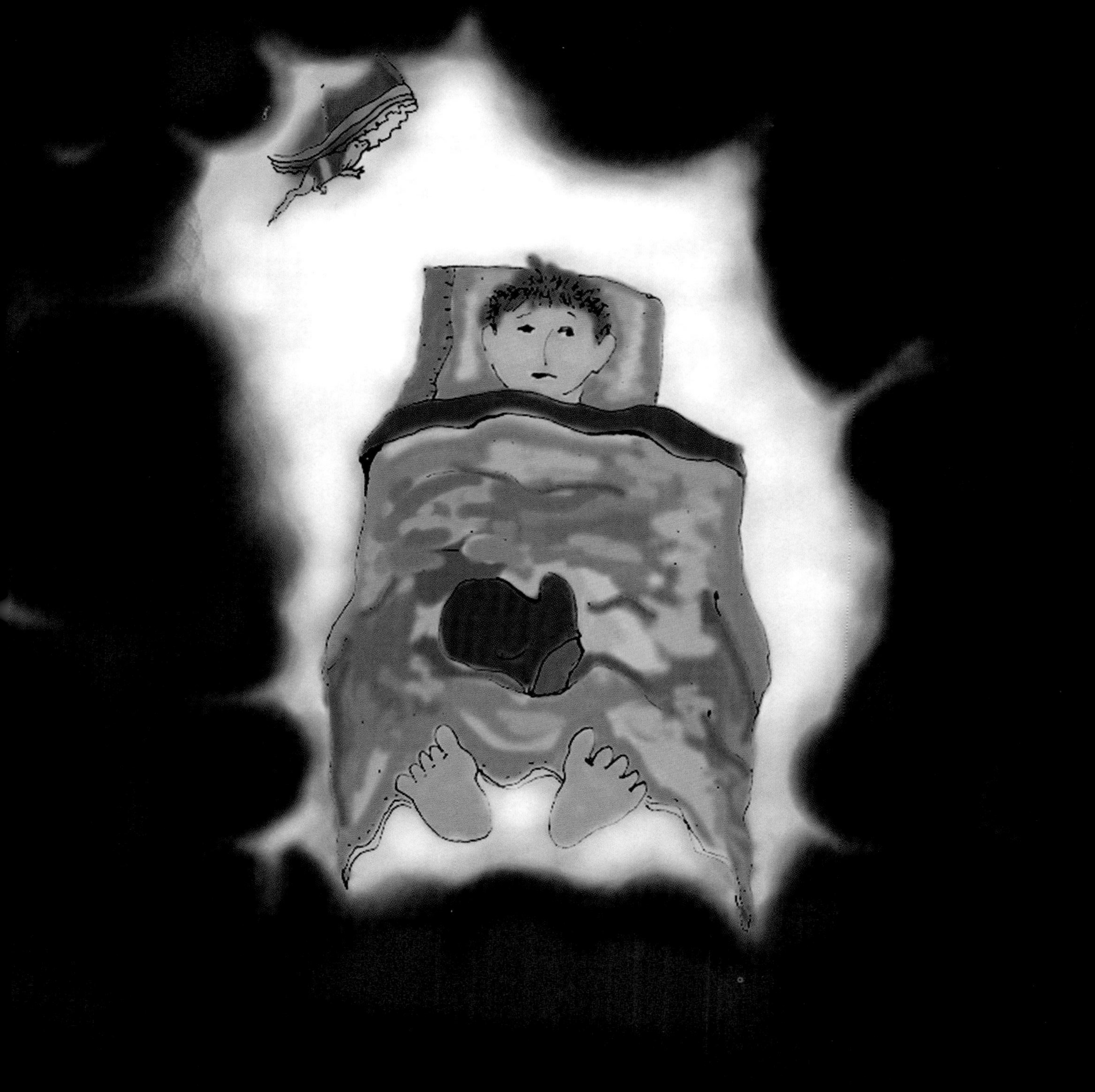

Just before waking up in the morning, Casey dreamt about a giant chameleon resting on his house.

In school the teacher started to read them a story called "The Little Prince." It was about a small prince who came from an asteroid in space. He landed on a new planet and made friends with a flower.

After he left the planet, the prince missed the flower and felt bad that he had left her with no one to care for her. A wise fox told the little prince that once you have nurtured something wild, you become responsible for it.

Remembering his dream Casey began checking his book bag. He took everything out, then looked through all the pockets. As he looked he imagined finding the chameleon at the bottom all squished from the weight of his science book. He imagined its little feet all flat and squashy looking.

He didn't notice that the teacher had stopped reading. He didn't notice that the teacher was no longer at her desk. He didn't notice that she was standing next to his desk. He finally did notice when she told him to stand up and march down to the principal's office to explain his behavior during reading. Casey wondered who first thought of remembering how to spell the word principal by repeating "The principal is your pal."

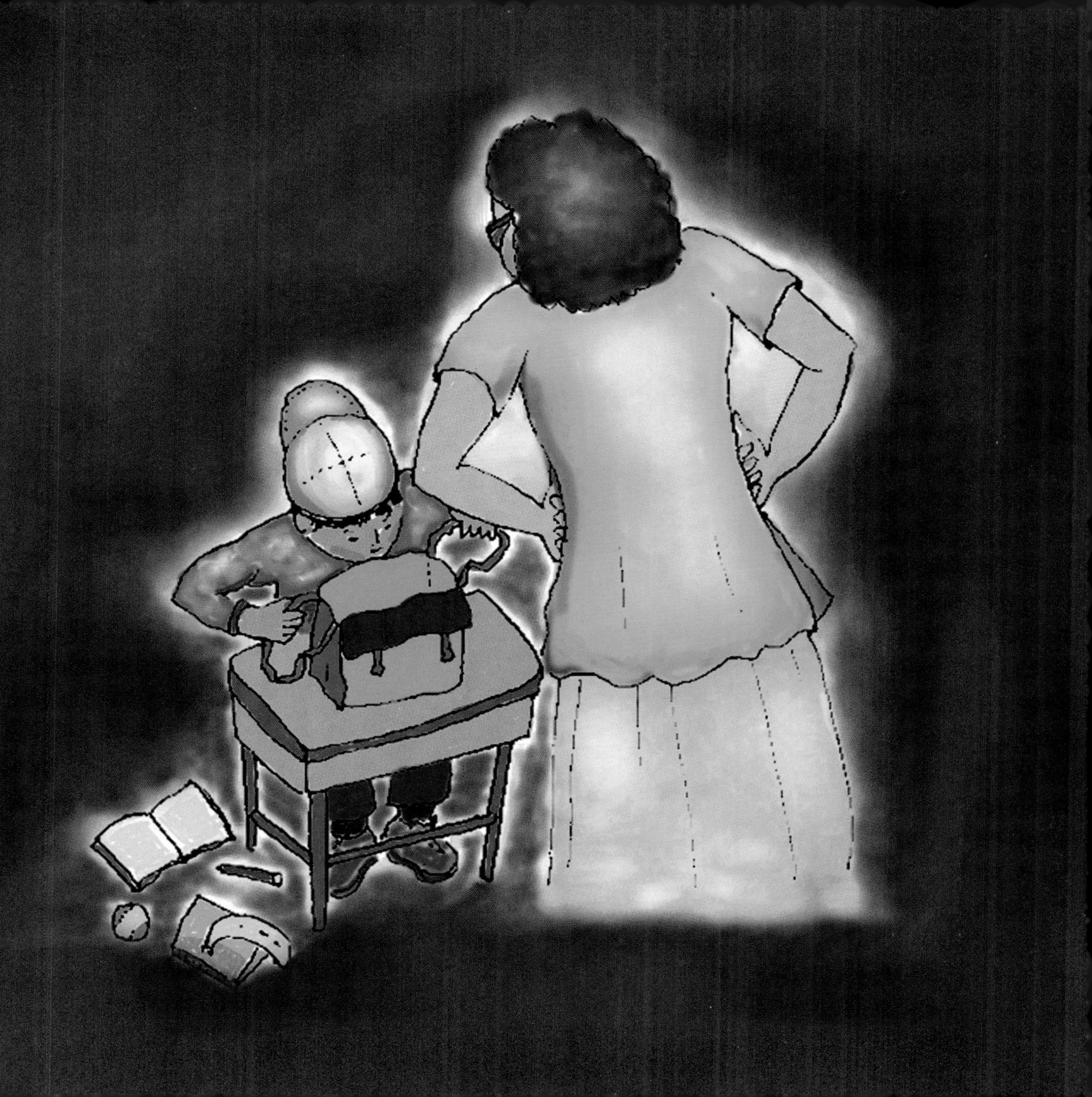

H
C

By the time Casey got home he was sure the chameleon was gone forever. He dropped his book bag by the front door before heading for his room.

Halfway up the stairs his mother's scream told him she had found his chameleon. He ran to his room to get the shoe box. Then he ran to the bathroom where his mom stood with her hands on her hips. "Young man..." she started but Casey was moving too fast.

He slid under the sink holding the shoe box up to where the chameleon clung to a pipe. Because its toes were wrapped around the pipe clinging tightly, he took the branch out of the shoe box and carefully unwound each toe from the pipe and then let the chameleon wrap its toes around the branch.

Casey put the branch back into the cardboard box. In seconds he was on the stairs and headed out the front door.

Casey ran all the way through the woods way back behind all the houses to a creek. When he reached the biggest fallen tree, where he had carved his initials last month, he stopped.

Casey thought about his giant chameleon dream. He remembered the words from "The Little Prince" about responsibility for wild things.

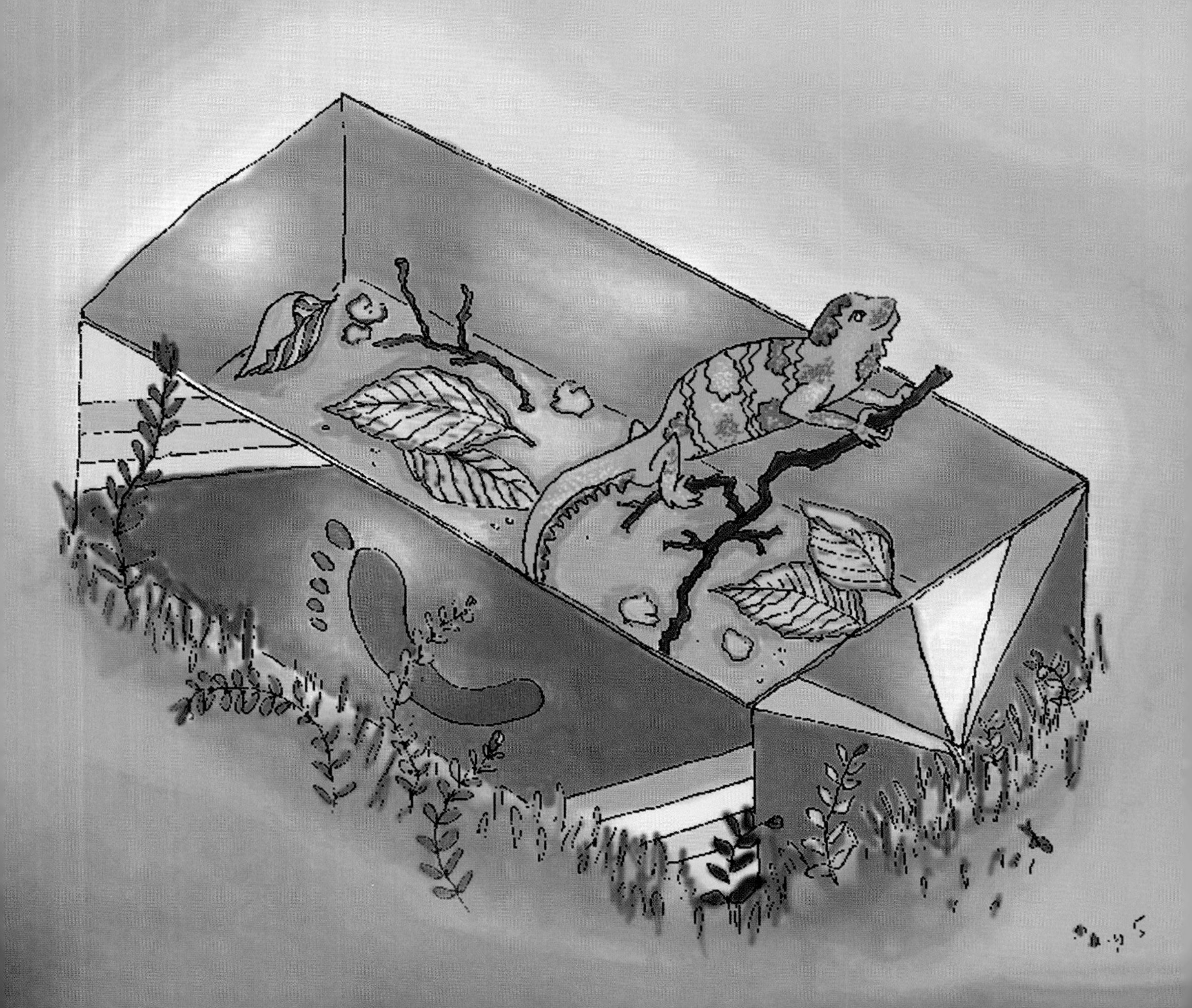

Slowly he opened the box a little. Two small eyes peered up at him from either side of the chameleon's head. Casey almost felt like crying. Of course he didn't.

Casey lifted the branch out of the box and laid it on a nearby bush. The chameleon slowly made its way to the top of the branch. The chameleon looked around before picking its way from the branch to the bush. Then it climbed to the top of the bush. It must have been very thirsty. It paused to raise its head under a large leaf that had a drop of water clinging to it. The chameleon opened its mouth and let the water drop down its throat.

Casey sat there for awhile thinking about stuff. Finally he climbed up on the tree trunk. He made two fists and flexed his muscles.

"I am the great prince of the ancient forest," he whispered. "I release you, Sir Chameleon, as my knight to guard the forest." He made a high-pitched shrieking sound before jumping off the tree trunk in a fine imitation of a flying squirrel, arms spread-eagled and legs wide apart.

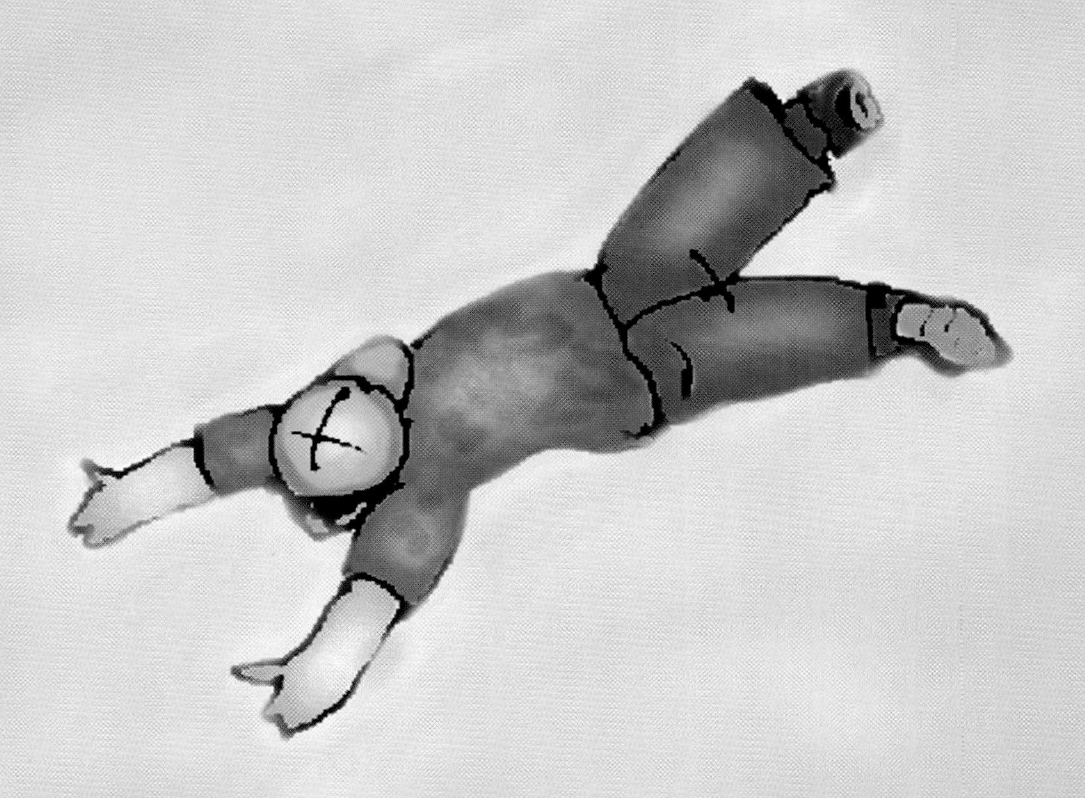

Supper at Casey's house was pretty quiet. Before it was over, Casey told his mom and dad that he was sorry about the chameleon and that he should have told them about it. He said he had found it by accident or he never would have brought it home. He said he would never do it again. He got up and went over to his mom and kissed her on the cheek. He said he was sorry his chameleon had scared her.

Then he took all the supper dishes into the kitchen and washed them. His mom and dad just looked at each other. His dad grinned. His mom touched her cheek where Casey had kissed her.

The next day Casey's dad brought home a young cockatiel. He told Casey that someone from work was getting transferred and couldn't take it with him. He said it would make a great pet. He told Casey that he could teach it to talk and do all kinds of tricks. So that's what Casey did.